Join Tiny in her miniature world
filled with BIG adventures!

TINY the Secret Adventurer

The Mystery Visitor

T0383291

First published in the UK in 2024 by Usborne Publishing Limited, Usborne House,

83-85 Saffron Hill, London EC1N 8RT, England. usborne.com

Usborne Verlag, Usborne Publishing Ltd., Prüfeninger Str. 20,
93049 Regensburg, Deutschland, VK Nr. 17560

Text copyright © Aisha Bushby, 2024

Illustrations by Kübra Teber © Usborne Publishing, Limited, 2024.

The name Usborne and the Balloon logo are trade marks of Usborne Publishing Limited.

A CIP catalogue record for this book is available from the British Library.

FMAMJJASOND/24 7640/1 ISBN 9781801314138

Printed and bound using 100% renewable energy at CPI Group (UK) Ltd, Croydon, CR0 4YY.

The
Mystery Visitor

Aisha Bushby

illustrated by Kübra Teber

USBORNE

Contents

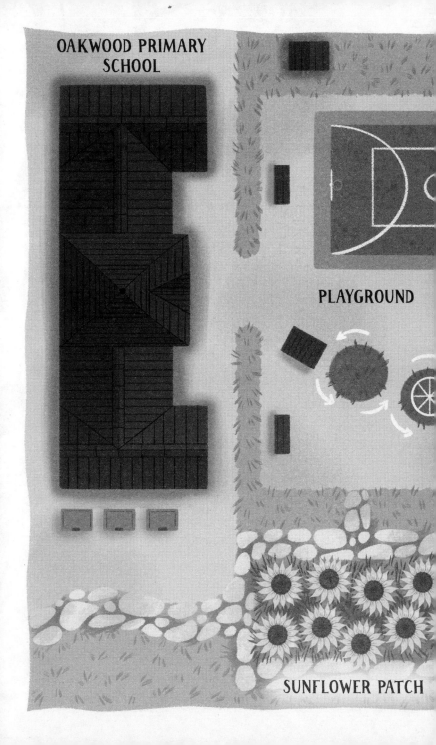

FROG'S HOLLOW

GARDEN SHED

WILDFLOWER MEADOW

VEGETABLE PATCH

WOODS

BLUEBERRY BUSH

GRASSLAND

CHAPTER 1

The Mystery Visitor

Tiny was staring up at the clouds, watching as they raced across the sky, when she felt the shock of cold water splashing her face. She sat up suddenly and shook her head. She was sitting at the centre of her sunflower, which was slightly tipped towards the sun. Tiny peered round to find out why she was so wet. Surrounding her

were bright yellow petals fanning upwards,
each of them carrying a raindrop from the
night before. It was a single raindrop that had
slid down one petal and onto Tiny's face.

Though a raindrop would hardly bother a human, it was enough to soak Tiny's hair. Because she wasn't a human at all. Even though she looked human – with arms and legs and hands and feet – she reached just the height of your forefinger.

Tiny looked like any human child might, with brown skin and eyes, and wavy brown hair.

But unlike a human child she wore bright sweet wrappers for clothes, which she made herself with whatever she found in the school garden where she lived.

Tiny could hear the birds chirp in the trees, cheerily welcoming another morning.

But she wasn't quite
ready for it herself.
It had been a long
night for her, as
something strange
and new rustled
in the grass.
She listened
to the birds'
updates to find
out what was
going on across the
garden and beyond.
They sat at a great
height and flew great

distances, and so they told
tales of places Tiny could
only imagine.

Tiny had never left
the school garden,
which consisted of
the sunflower patch,
grassland and woods,
where her friend
Squirrel lived.
Beyond that was the
vegetable patch and
wildflower meadow,
leading to the pond
where her other friend,

Frog, lived. In between were lots of other creatures, the sort that humans might not notice because they live between blades of grass, or inside shrubs. There were spiders and slugs; woodlice and worms; and mice that skittered and scattered at the sound of any movement.

The garden was in the grounds of Oakwood Primary School, where children came to learn each day. Tiny and her friends knew to stay away from the playground, where the children gathered at the sound of a great big bell. But there was one child Tiny quite liked: Nour.

She had planted Tiny's sunflower.

She tended to it lovingly each day, and afterwards she often sat nearby, reading a book that Tiny would secretly glance at. In a way, Tiny felt like Nour was her friend.

After the bell rang each morning and Nour went inside with the other children, Tiny liked to hear what the birds had to say.

But today, as the playground emptied, they said something that alarmed her. "Have you heard?" said one bird.

"Heard what?" asked another.

Tiny had to listen extra carefully because they whispered the next part, and she only caught a few words of what they were saying. But each one was more frightening than the last. "Mysterious creature..."

"Sharp claws...scary fangs..."

That was enough for Tiny to decide she had to do some investigating. She slipped between the sunflower's petals and climbed carefully down its stem, using each leaf as a stepladder. When she was close enough, she leaped to the ground.

Tiny decided to visit her friend Squirrel first. Squirrel lived in the tree next to the birds, so she might know what the birds were whispering about. Maybe, together, Tiny and Squirrel could find out more about their mystery visitor.

CHAPTER 2

Tiny Investigates

It was a long walk to Squirrel's, and Tiny made sure to nibble on a seed and sip on a raindrop before she left. She would need to cross the sunflower patch before making it to the grassland that came before the woods where Squirrel lived.

A sunflower was as tall as a tree to Tiny, but she could recognize each one by

19

the colour of its stem, or the shape of its leaves. *Her* sunflower stood out to her the most, even though it was the smallest.

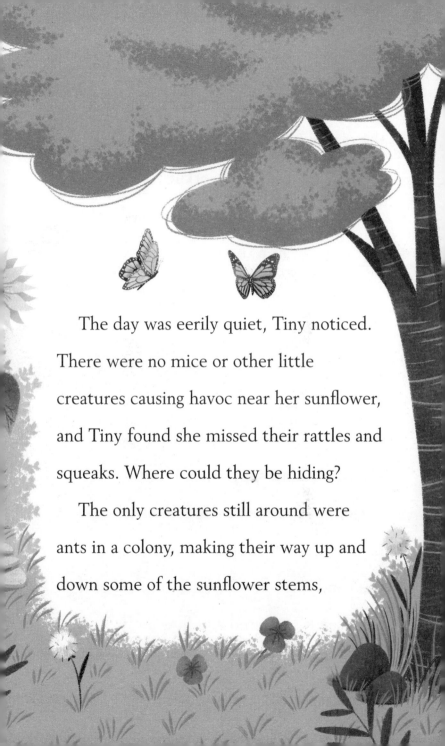

The day was eerily quiet, Tiny noticed. There were no mice or other little creatures causing havoc near her sunflower, and Tiny found she missed their rattles and squeaks. Where could they be hiding?

The only creatures still around were ants in a colony, making their way up and down some of the sunflower stems, and the bees who were busy pollinating the plants. They rarely stopped to chat – they were too busy working.

Whatever the creature was, it didn't seem to threaten them.

In the silence, Tiny could hear each of her footsteps crunch against the earth. There were some big pebbles dotted around the grassland. It would be difficult for her to climb over and round each pebble without slipping and hurting herself, so she used a dandelion stalk to help her. Tiny held onto it tight, and let the wind carry her forward, until all of its little seeds scattered and flew away.

She landed right in the middle of the grassland. The grass was still wet after the rain and smelled sharp and sweet. Tiny enjoyed the feeling of the grass as it tickled her cheeks.

Up ahead were the woods where Squirrel lived, and it was a challenge for Tiny to make her way through the taller blades of grass. She had to be careful to lift her legs up high.

Even though Tiny was busy looking at where to step next, she didn't notice the ground dip suddenly, and she tripped and fell into a hole.

Except, when Tiny stood up and dusted herself down she saw it wasn't a hole at all, but a giant paw print. It had rained the night before and so the print was carved neatly into the wet soil.

The blades of grass and clovers around

the paw print were crushed, as if beneath a great weight. Across from the triangular dip of the paw pad were four smaller ovals, and piercing holes just above each one.

That was Tiny's first sign that they had a mysterious visitor in the school garden. There was another sign of the visitor that gave Tiny a clue as to what it could be – a tuft of bright orange fur.

If Tiny could just get to Squirrel, tell her about the paw print and show her the fur, her friend might be able to help her piece these clues together to work out who the visitor was.

She collected the tuft of fur for evidence, and tucked it into her belt. Then she crept forward slowly and quietly, in case the creature was nearby.

It was while she was creeping forward that she saw another paw print and realized that the creature had been heading towards the woods... towards Squirrel.

Then, Tiny heard a scream that she recognized all too well.

"Squirrel!" Tiny yelled. "Squirrel, I'm on my way!" Tiny sprinted through the grass, picking her legs up high. She was no longer worried about being quiet as she raced to save her friend.

CHAPTER 3

Squirrel's Fruit

Crossing the grassland to the woods would
only take a few strides for a human child,
but for Tiny it was like running the length
of an entire football field.

Her sides ached as she sprinted, tripping
over loose soil along the way. She grazed
her arms and knocked her knees, but she
couldn't stop until she reached her friend.

Tiny hadn't really thought what she would do if she encountered the mystery visitor, but she decided she'd figure that out when she came to it. She kept going, another colony of ants dancing out of her way, a bee buzzing to a surprised halt above her.

Finally, Tiny entered the mouth of the woods. The trees reached higher than Tiny could see, disappearing into a cloud of green.

"Help!" Squirrel called from nearby. She sounded more distressed than Tiny had ever heard her before. Tiny glimpsed into the gloom of the trees where not much sunlight reached, and spotted her friend – grey fur standing on end – lying between the trunks of two trees.

"Squirrel, I'm here!" Tiny said breathlessly, and she rushed over to Squirrel. Aside from her grey fur, Squirrel had two fluffy pointed ears and a fluffier tail. Little claw-like hands and feet were tucked at

her sides and, right now, her big
front teeth were on show as she
cried out for help.

"Oh, Tiny, I'm so glad to see you!" said Squirrel, rolling around on the ground.

"Are you hurt?" asked Tiny, alarmed.

Squirrel nodded pitifully. "In my belly."

Tiny checked Squirrel's belly, afraid she'd been wounded, but there didn't seem to be anything wrong.

"Your belly looks fine," said Tiny, a little confused. "Did the creature attack you?"

"Creature?" said Squirrel. "Did *it* steal my fruit?" Suddenly she sat up, her tail bristling in anger. "Where is it? I'll teach it a lesson…I'll…I'll—"

"Squirrel!" Tiny interrupted, waving her hands in front of her face to get Squirrel's attention. "Can you *please* explain what is going on and why your belly hurts if the creature hasn't attacked you?"

Squirrel let out an angry puff. "*Someone* has stolen my fruit, and so my belly hurts because I'm hungry. I haven't eaten since dawn!"

"Oh," said Tiny, letting out a relieved sigh. "Oh, Squirrel, I thought you were hurt!"

"I am!" said Squirrel. "If I don't eat soon it'll be the end of me!" With that, Squirrel keeled over again and let out a dramatic wail.

"Can't you…just find more fruit?" Tiny suggested.

Squirrel opened an eye to peek at Tiny. "I bet it was those horrible little human creatures," she said, ignoring Tiny's suggestion.

"They're not so bad, really," said Tiny.

Most of the schoolchildren tended to the flowers so gently, she couldn't imagine them being horrible.

"Yes they are!" insisted Squirrel. "They're always taking over my woods. Building forts and running round my trees. And now they've stolen *my* fruit."

"Well, Squirrel, they're not exactly *your* woods, are they?"

Tiny was going to explain, patiently, that they had to share their home. But Squirrel was glaring at her so fiercely she decided to try something else.

"Why don't we check in with the mice? I'll ask them about the creature, and you ask them if they know what happened to your fruit. Then we can check in with the birds. They'll know the most, I'm sure of it."

Squirrel paused. "That idea sounds far too sensible... But I'll try it."

With that, Tiny climbed on her friend's back and clung onto her soft, grey fur. Her stomach jolted as Squirrel skittered between the trees to find the mice.

CHAPTER 4

The Mice

Tiny heard the mice before she saw them.
They were chanting a strange poem, only
stopping to giggle and cheer.

What is going on? Tiny wondered.
The mice had a habit of playing games
they copied from the children in the
playground. She wondered if that was
what they were doing now.

Squirrel skittered through a large berry bush and, as the leaves parted, they both entered a clearing where the mice were gathered.

"Oh," was all Tiny said, as she tried to make sense of what she was seeing. The mice were sitting in a circle, facing one another, while one mouse walked round and chanted, "Duck, duck…

GOOSE!"

As the mouse paced round they tapped each of the other mice on the head, calling out, "Duck!". If they called out, "Goose!" the mouse they had tapped on the head stood up and chased them. They ran round once, then the mouse sat in the space the "goose" had left.

"You lose!" said the mouse cheerily.

Then the next mouse walked round the circle, chanting, "Duck, duck, goose!"

Tiny and Squirrel watched as the mice

played several more rounds of the game. Sometimes, the mouse who had been called a goose would catch the first mouse before they sat down. And the first mouse would have to call, "Duck, duck, goose," again, until they could find a seat.

The last time Tiny had asked the mice if she could play one of their playground games with them, they said no. But this time when she asked, they made their circle larger.

"How exciting!" said Tiny, sitting down with them and secretly hoping she would be the next goose. And she was!

She stood up, chasing the mouse round the circle. Tiny was faster, but the mouse had a head start and managed to grab Tiny's spot before she could catch them. It was thrilling!

Tiny was secretly glad she had lost, because it meant *she* could have a turn at picking the next "goose."

The school bell came and went, and so
did the children. But Tiny was so intent on
playing her game, she barely noticed them.
And anyway, the mice were well hidden.

45

No one would find them here. While Tiny played, Squirrel busied herself gathering berries and filling her belly.

Eventually, Tiny remembered why she'd come to find the mice, and she asked if they would pause the game for a moment so she could speak to them.

"Squirrel and I are here because—"

"We want to know who stole my fruit!" Squirrel interrupted. "I've carefully marked my trees and bushes, and everyone knows not to pick any fruit from them."

Tiny turned to her, sighing. She thought it best for Squirrel to get her question out of the way first. Squirrel could be stubborn when she had her mind on something.

"It wasn't me!" said one mouse.

"Nor me!" said another.

"I bet the birds took it…" said a third
mouse. Their mothers scolded them for
accusing the birds without having any
evidence. "…Or maybe they didn't."

"We'll be speaking to the birds next,"
said Tiny. "Thank you." She glanced over at
Squirrel to see if her friend was satisfied.
Then she said, "I had a question too."

That was when Tiny told the mice about
what she'd heard the birds whispering. She
described the paw print and showed them
the tuft of fur in her belt.

"That looks a bit like Squirrel's fur," said the mouse that had just been told off. "Look, she's got orange patches in between the grey."

"How dare you!" said Squirrel, offended. "I would know my own fur, and this fur is longer than mine."

Tiny nodded, thankful her friend was being helpful. "It's true. Look here."

The mice gathered and peered more closely at the fur.

Then, one of the quieter mice said, "I...I did find this earlier." The mouse dragged over a whisker. "It's not one of our whiskers, because ours are much smaller."

Tiny inspected the whisker, which was as long as she was tall. The mice were right. What creature could it belong to? Whatever it was, it must be a large animal to have such a big whisker.

"Can I keep this?" Tiny asked. The mouse nodded and Tiny slid the whisker into her belt. "Thank you, you've been really helpful."

"And if you find out who stole my fruit," added Squirrel, "tell them I'm *not* happy about it."

CHAPTER 5

The Birds

Next, Tiny jumped on Squirrel's back
and they returned to the woods together,
where they planned to speak to the birds.
They moved so quickly through the grass
that Squirrel accidentally flew through an
abandoned spider's web. She managed to
pull most of the web off herself, but some
of it stuck to Tiny's skin and hair.

"Oh, how weird!" Tiny said, peering
down at the shimmering silk. "It's…
beautiful."

They paused for a moment to rub it
off themselves, rolling around in the grass,
before continuing on. Eventually, Squirrel
settled at the base of a massive tree.

"Are you ready to go up, Tiny? It'll be much higher than your sunflower."

Tiny paused, staring up the impossibly high tree. Suddenly, her legs felt funny and her belly gurgled. But not because she was hungry – she was afraid.

"I-I think so," said Tiny.

The words were barely out of her mouth before Squirrel leaped straight up, climbing the tree trunk at lightning speed. Tiny fell backwards, almost falling to the ground, but she managed to keep hold of Squirrel. She wrapped both arms round Squirrel's neck, like she was giving her friend a big hug.

Tiny had to admit it was fun leaping from branch to branch to find the birds. The leaves whizzed by Tiny, and she let out a whoop that was both delighted and fearful as they climbed higher and higher and higher.

Eventually, Squirrel settled on a branch halfway up the tree, and Tiny could finally see the view.

From her sunflower, Tiny had been able to see each side of the school garden. But from here in the trees she could see well beyond it. There were rows of buildings for miles around, surrounded by green fields. There were humans far below, in the streets next to the school garden. From this height, they looked the same size as Tiny.

Before she could look around more, the birds interrupted them.

"What are *you* doing here?" they said, glaring at Tiny and Squirrel. "This is *our*

tree, Squirrel.
If you won't
let us near
yours,
then the
same rules
should apply
here."

"And,"
said another bird,
"*she* isn't even a tree dweller." They turned
a beady eye on Tiny. Even though the
school garden animals had accepted her as
one of their own, the birds could be a little
grumpy.

"We're here," said Squirrel, before Tiny had the chance to show them the evidence she'd collected on her belt, "to find out who stole my fruit. Was it you?" asked Squirrel, peering at one bird. "Or was it *you*?" she said, leaning towards another.

Some of the school garden animals disliked Squirrel because they found her a little too energetic. She often panicked, moved quite quickly, and was forever dropping nuts on them without apologizing. But Tiny understood that it was just her nature, and that everyone has flaws.

The most important thing was that Squirrel (when she was well fed) was the kindest friend.

Squirrel was the first animal in the school garden to give Tiny a chance, and she often carried Tiny around to help her move over longer distances. Tiny was glad to have a friend like Squirrel.

"We have no interest in your fruit," said one of the birds. "We have plenty of food on *our* side of the woods. Now, will you please leave?"

Tiny decided it was her time to speak. "Excuse me," she said, climbing off Squirrel's back. She stood, on her own, beneath three towering birds. If they'd wanted to, they could have plucked her up like she was a worm. Still, Tiny didn't let this worry her. She had to find out who the mystery visitor was. "I wanted to show you something. I heard you talking about a mysterious creature earlier, and I've collected some…evidence."

Tiny pulled from her belt the tuft of orange fur. The birds gathered closer, curious.

"Yes, the creature I saw was orange!"
said one of the birds. "I was out getting
some worms just after sunrise, when
something leaped at me."

Tiny thought that sounded very dangerous and scary. The other birds comforted the first bird, who seemed to enjoy the attention.

Tiny waited for a moment, until they calmed down. Then, she pulled out the sleek whisker.

"How do we know that isn't your fur?" said another bird, glancing at Tiny's hair.

"It's too long to be mine," said Tiny, holding it up against her head. "And it's thicker, too."

"Hmph," said the birds, eventually agreeing with her. Finally, Tiny described the paw print she'd seen. While she was chatting with the birds, Squirrel busily munched on a few twigs.

"Orange fur, long whisker, paw prints…" said one of the birds, deep in thought.

"Didn't you say you'd seen fangs and bright yellow eyes, too?" said another bird to its friend.

"Oh, yes I did!" answered the first bird that had spoken. The birds put their heads together to think which creature could fit the description.

"Well?" said Tiny impatiently. "What could those things belong to?" She'd only ever met the school garden animals before, so she had no way of guessing who their mystery visitor was. But the birds often travelled long distances; they'd seen much more of the world than Tiny. If anyone could guess who the mysterious creature was, it would be them.

"I think it's a cat," said one of the birds, finally.

"I disagree," said another bird. "It's more likely a dog."

"A dog? How silly. They never go anywhere without a human attached to them."

"No, no, it's neither of those. It's definitely a—"

But before the third bird could finish saying who *they* thought the mystery visitor was, Squirrel interrupted with a shriek. "There it is! I've seen it. I've seen the mysterious creature!"

CHAPTER 6

Saving Frog

"What?" said Tiny, turning round so quickly that she almost fell off the branch. She hurriedly climbed on top of Squirrel's back for a better look. "Where, Squirrel? Where is it?"

"There, Tiny!" said Squirrel. "There's something in the wildflower meadow. Look."

At first, all Tiny could see were the flowers blooming in a rainbow of colour, and the fruit and vegetable patch next to them. But then she noticed that some of the flowers looked as if they were dancing. But they weren't dancing at all; it was just that a large creature was stalking through them. Tiny saw a tuft of orange fur and the points of two triangular ears.

Further behind, a long fluffy tail was swaying left and right, like a pendulum. The tail had a white tip, as if it had been dipped in snow.

"Oh no!" said Tiny, looking beyond the mysterious creature to where it was heading.

There, sitting on a lily pad in his pond, was
Frog, completely unaware of the creature
that was coming his way.

"Frog!" Tiny and Squirrel called at the
same time. Tiny waved her arms. "Frog!"
they called even louder.

The

mysterious

creature's

ears

pricked

up, as if it

had heard

them too.

It stood up

and turned, looking right at Tiny. It had

shining yellow eyes like stars. And then it

crouched down and carried on creeping

towards Frog.

After they called his name for the third

time, Frog finally spotted them.

"Tiny? Squirrel? Is that
you?" Frog called,
waving an arm
at his friends.
"Hello!
Come for
a swim."

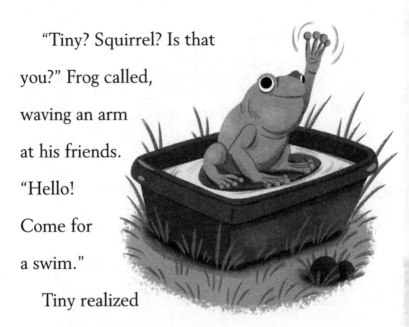

Tiny realized
that Frog thought they were
greeting him, not warning him.

"No!" called Tiny, and she started
pointing towards the wildflower meadow.

Frog paused for a moment, then left his
pond and hopped forward. "What did you
say? Hang on, I'll come to you."

"No!" Tiny cried, turning to Squirrel. "We have to stop him before he gets too close to the creature. Who knows what it'll do to him?"

Tiny and Squirrel whizzed down the tree and towards Frog's Hollow, hoping they would reach their friend before the creature did. In her rush, Tiny left the fur and whisker behind – but she didn't need them now she'd solved the mystery.

CHAPTER 7

Tiny in Trouble

Soil exploded in the air and vegetable roots crumbled beneath Squirrel's feet as they skittered across the fruit and vegetable patch. At one point, Tiny nearly fell off Squirrel's back again, the rush of wind loosening her grip on Squirrel's fur.

By the time Tiny and Squirrel reached Frog, they'd lost sight of the creature.

Peering behind her, Tiny could no longer see its ears and tail poking out of the flowers.

"Hello Tiny, hello Squirrel!" said Frog, looking both surprised and pleased to see his friends. "I didn't think you'd heard me invite you for a swim. I was just making my way round to you when we bumped into each other."

"Well, you didn't come *round* really,"
Squirrel pointed out. "You went in a
straight line through—"

"Squirrel," Tiny interrupted. "We need
to be extra quiet right now."

She climbed down from her friend's
back, landing on the wetter mud that
surrounded Frog's pond.

Everyone fell silent, and Tiny could feel
her heart pitter-pattering at the thought of
the mysterious creature's arrival.

"What's going on?" whispered Frog, his
excitement turning to worry.

Tiny turned back to check whether
the creature was still lurking. Everything

was quiet, but she was worried they
didn't have much time. She told Frog
everything she had discovered that day
about the mysterious creature: the tuft of
fur, the paw print, the whisker. She even

mentioned the fangs and yellow eyes, and finally how she had glimpsed the creature in the wildflower meadow.

As she finished, Tiny heard a rustle that sounded like the padding of giant paws.

Following that came a low growl.

"Oh," said Frog, looking afraid. "Oh no, oh no. Watch out!" He retreated further into his pond, hiding beneath his lily pad.

Squirrel's tail bristled as she stood behind Tiny.

The rustling in the bushes grew louder and louder and louder until…

As quick as lightning, the creature leaped. All Tiny saw was a flash of its bright yellow eyes before everything went dark.

It took her a moment to understand what had happened. The creature had gobbled her up whole.

CHAPTER 8

Poor Thing

It was dark in the creature's mouth, and Tiny could feel its smooth fangs clamped shut in front of her, like a cage. From behind she could hear the growl coming from its belly, which rumbled and quaked. Its tongue wasn't soft and slimy, but rough. Tiny felt as though she was brushed up against wet bark.

And the smell was something Tiny had never experienced before. Pungent and sour.

Tiny, however, wasn't going to give up without a fight. She raised her arms above her head and pushed with all her might, trying to lift the mysterious creature's jaw open. But Tiny was too small and much

weaker than the creature to make
a difference.

It was starting to get hot, and Tiny
began to feel dizzy. She could tell that the
creature was moving, jolting left and right,
throwing her around like she had been
caught in a gust of wind.

Whenever Frog or Squirrel had a
problem, Tiny was usually good at solving
it. Like the time Frog's pond was flipped
upside down and today when Squirrel
had lost her fruit. But it was hard to think
when so much was happening at once.

Eventually, Tiny fell backwards, almost
slipping down into the creature's belly.

She grabbed onto something long and slimy at the back of its throat. The creature stopped moving and made a sound that was like a whisper, or a hiss.

Tiny felt a whoosh of air and a force even stronger than wind pushed her out of the creature's mouth and back into the sunlight.

Tiny fell into a great clump of grass, drinking in the sweet air. When she looked at the creature again she could see it was bent down, choking. Its ears were laid back and its tongue was sticking out of its mouth. Its yellow eyes were wide with surprise and fear.

After a while the creature calmed down
and turned to Tiny.

Her first instinct was to run and hide,
but then the creature spoke and said
something that Tiny did not expect.

"You taste gross."

Tiny pulled

herself up

straight

and stared

into its

eyes with a

scowl. "Well,

I didn't have much

fun in your mouth either. It stinks! What made you think you could put me in there without asking?"

The creature's ears peeled back in surprise.

"I'm sorry," it said. "I'm a fox, you see,

and I usually eat meat, but I haven't eaten anything in days and I'm just so hungry. I saw some fruit in the woods earlier, but it wasn't enough to fill my belly. Then I saw a bird, but it was too quick for me. So when I saw the frog too, well… I'm still only a cub but I think my instincts are kicking in…"

The creature did a lot of talking, quite quickly, and Tiny had to concentrate hard to keep up with it.

"Your fur is really pretty," Tiny exclaimed, when the fox finally took a breath. She couldn't help but admire how bright it was.

"Oh," said the fox. "Thank you. Well, anyway, I'm not so good at hunting… I caught you instead of the frog! But as soon as I had you in my mouth, I knew

something wasn't right. Those strange

things on your body," it said, pointing its

nose at Tiny's clothes, "they didn't

feel right."

"I would have spat you back out right away," the fox continued. "But your friends chased me and so I panicked and ran. They're a little scary, you know. Even the frog, when he wants to be."

Now that Tiny had spent a few minutes talking to the fox, she was no longer afraid of it. It was much smaller than it seemed and it had scratches on its ears that looked a little sore.

Tiny heard another rustle in the bushes, followed by a terrifying croak. There, tearing through the grass was Squirrel with Frog on her back. Frog was responsible for the scary noises, and Squirrel had a bunch

of pebbles which
she catapulted
at the fox.

Before
Tiny could
ask her
friends to stop
and allow the fox
to explain itself to them,
it crouched down and let out a pitiful bark.
Then, it disappeared into the depths of the
wildflower meadow.

"We did it, Tiny!" said Squirrel
excitedly.

"We saved you," said Frog, proudly.

They each danced round her to celebrate.

"Oh," said Tiny, looking behind her at where the fox had been. Then she whispered quietly, so her friends couldn't hear, "Poor thing."

CHAPTER 9

Tiny's Plan

Squirrel and Frog gathered some armour for Tiny, insisting she wear it until they were sure the creature had gone for good. When she returned to her sunflower, she had an acorn as a helmet and an empty snail's shell around her body.

She thought she looked silly, but her friends wouldn't listen to her protests, so she did as they asked.

"You can sleep by my pond!" Frog suggested.

"Or in my tree," Squirrel offered.

But it had been a long day, and all Tiny wanted to do was return to her sunflower. So she politely declined their sleepover offers, agreeing to let Squirrel drop her off at her sunflower at dusk.

But once she laid down, no matter how tired her body was (even her ears and nose were aching), her mind was whirring like a bumblebee's wings. Tiny tossed and turned for hours up on her flower, wondering what had happened to the fox.

"I know it tried to attack Frog and eat
me… And the birds and the mice and all
the other animals were hiding from it. Still
I can't help but think it didn't *mean* to be
bad. It was just hungry."

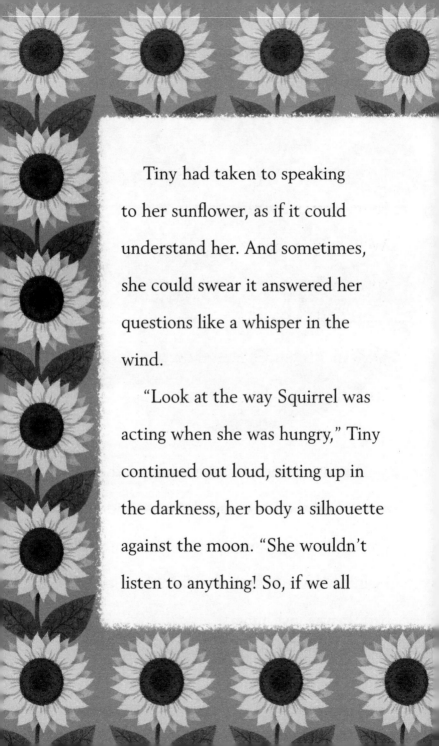

Tiny had taken to speaking to her sunflower, as if it could understand her. And sometimes, she could swear it answered her questions like a whisper in the wind.

"Look at the way Squirrel was acting when she was hungry," Tiny continued out loud, sitting up in the darkness, her body a silhouette against the moon. "She wouldn't listen to anything! So, if we all just listened to the fox and tried to understand what it needed… Well, maybe then it wouldn't be so scary."

Tiny thought about how the birds and Squirrel argued over their trees, and how Squirrel was always accusing everyone of stealing her food. But in spite of all of that, they were a family, living in the school garden together. And even though Tiny was different, they accepted her. She often guided the bumblebees to the right flowers, and invited the mice up to the sunflowers to watch the moon.

And Tiny was sure that, given the chance, the fox would offer something too.

"Thank you, Tiny," said a voice.

Tiny jumped, nearly falling off her sunflower in surprise, knocking off all her armour. Her heart swooped in her chest, like a hunting bird, as she sat up to see who had spoken.

She looked across at the flowers but couldn't see anything at that height. It was only when she glanced down that she saw

two familiar yellow eyes peering at her from the gloom.

"Oh, it's you!" Tiny said, relieved to see the fox again. "You stayed after all."

She slowly climbed back down her sunflower onto the soil, and the fox watched her patiently, its eyes following her all the way.

When Tiny landed, she peered up at it.

"What are you doing up so late?" Tiny asked.

Many of the animals in the garden were fast asleep, and Tiny whispered to make sure she didn't wake anyone up.

"I'm a fox," explained the fox, even though Tiny already knew that. "And so I'm nocturnal."

"What does that mean?" asked Tiny.

"It means I stay up at night and sleep during the day. I won't be a nuisance, I promise," it said, ears back, head stooped low. "I really shouldn't have been up earlier. I was hungry and, well…"

Before the fox could continue speaking,

its belly rumbled and Tiny could see the glow disappear from its eyes, like fading stars.

"I'm sorry," the fox said eventually.

Tiny watched it for a moment, and an idea began to form in her mind. "You've already apologized," she said. "But I think I have a solution to your hunger problems that all of the school garden animals might be happy with..."

CHAPTER 10

Delicious

The fox lay flat on the ground, allowing Tiny to climb onto its back. Its fur was a little like Squirrel's, though longer and fluffier, like a cloud. Tiny directed it left and right, until they reached the school bins just to the side of the main building. She hoped they might find some leftover food there.

They each stared up at the bin, and
Tiny thought the leftovers didn't smell
too appealing. They made her turn up her
nose, but they seemed to entice the fox
forward.

"Go on," Tiny encouraged. "Set me down, then climb in and have a look!"

Tiny watched as the fox climbed stacks of boxes piled high, before jumping the rest of the way to the top of the bin.

"That was very impressive!" Tiny called from below, but she wasn't sure the fox heard her,

because it had disappeared inside the bin.
A few moments passed. Tiny heard rustling
and scraping noises and, as she waited, she
worried that her new friend wouldn't be
able to get back out of the bin again. But
then, like a bolt of lightning, the fox landed
in front of her without a sound, a big bite
of food in its mouth.

"You're so quiet!" Tiny said, impressed.
"No wonder all the animals were scared.
You're very good at creeping up on
creatures."

"Thank you," the fox said through the
mouthful of food it was carrying. It placed
the food on the ground and sniffed at it,

before giving it a tentative lick and then a hungry bite. The fox ate whatever its food was quickly, making guzzling noises with its throat. Then it licked its lips several times.

"That was delicious!" the fox said. "The best food I've ever had."

Tiny grinned. "Oh, I'm so glad!"

Then she felt a little sad. How would she convince the rest of the school garden that the fox was good? It reminded her a little of when she'd been new to the garden, and how she'd tried to fit in.

The fox decided to raid the bins one more time for a second helping of food, before returning Tiny to her sunflower.

Climbing up the stem, she peered at the stars once more. Only when she came up with a plan for the next day did Tiny drift off into a deep and restful sleep.

CHAPTER 11

A New Friend

"Are you *sure* this is a good idea?" the fox asked the next morning, as Tiny climbed onto its back and settled in its soft fur.

"No," admitted Tiny, feeling nervous, but it was too late to turn back now. All the school garden animals were waiting for her in the wildflower meadow, where she had asked for a meeting. They didn't know, however, that the fox would be attending too.

The good thing was, no one was around as Tiny and the fox trotted to the wildflower meadow, and so they didn't have any nasty surprises along the way. But the bad news was that when Tiny and the fox finally arrived, the animals panicked all at once.

The birds tittered and took to the nearest tree, the mice hid and Squirrel and Frog looked as if they were about to attack the fox again. But Tiny climbed on top of its soft head and spoke as loudly and as confidently as she could.

"Thank you, everyone, for meeting me here today," she began.

"What's going on?" asked an angry bird.

"Tiny, blink once to let us know you're okay up there!" said a mouse. "And twice if you're in trouble." This was followed by a low, panicked murmur. "That's three blinks! What do three blinks mean?"

The other animals started to panic again until both Squirrel and Frog hushed them.

"Tiny is trying to speak," said Frog, sternly, moving to join Tiny to the left of the fox.

"Yes," added Squirrel, moving to join Tiny to the right of the fox, though her body was shaking a little. "She called this meeting, so it must be important; we should listen."

Tiny grinned at her friends and whispered a thank you. She was so pleased that they trusted her.

Back on the ground again, Tiny turned
to the other animals, who were half hidden
among the flowers, ready to run.

"I know there's been word of a
mysterious creature," Tiny said. She could
hear the fox's heart beating loudly, and

saw its ears pulled back. Everyone was
watching them closely. "Well, he isn't
mysterious at all but a new friend."

"Ludicrous!" shouted a bird, flapping its wings crossly. Tiny knew now wasn't the right time to ask what the word meant, but she could tell it wasn't a *good* one from the way the bird ruffled its feathers.

"Quiet!" said Frog, in warning, and he croaked so loudly that the animals fell silent again.

"What I mean to say," Tiny continued, struggling with her words, but then she thought to give some examples. "Birds, didn't I help you when Squirrel said you stole her food? And, mice, what about those times I invited you all to visit my sunflower?"

No one interrupted this time, and so Tiny took a deep breath and continued.

"When I first arrived, none of you liked me, did you?" She peered at the animals with her hardest stare, her brown eyes shining. "You said I looked like a human and so you thought I would destroy the school garden. But has that happened?"

One by one, the animals shook their heads.

Tiny nodded. "Exactly. You judged me before knowing me."

Everyone was silent. Some of the smaller mice were sniffling, their eyes wet.

"Er," whispered Frog. "Let's maybe end on a positive note?"

"Oh! Oops," said Tiny. "You're right.

Erm… But now… Well, now look at us!
We're such good friends."

The mice nodded tearfully. "It's true!"
they said. "We love you, Tiny!"

"So," Tiny finished, "I'm just asking you
to accept our new friend… Erm… Oh,
what *is* your name?" she asked the fox,
peering up at it.

"Oh, well, what's yours?" the fox asked
Frog and Squirrel. They explained that
their names were Frog and Squirrel. "Okay,
then, well, I guess mine is…Fox!"

"Wonderful," said Tiny. "I'm just asking you all accept Fox."

And then Tiny recounted their adventure from the night before and explained that Fox would mostly be awake at night and asleep during the day (this seemed to please the birds). She also explained that Fox would keep watch over the littler animals in the dark (this seemed to please the mice) and help them find food when they needed it (this pleased Squirrel, who immediately asked Fox to help her gather some fruit).

After Tiny was finished, some of the animals had questions.

"Your fur is beautiful," said Frog. Fox dipped his head bashfully in response. "Orange is my second favourite colour," Frog continued. "Green is my first, obviously."

"You won't steal our berries, will you?" asked the mice. "Or eat us?" They were satisfied when Fox said no to both.

"Where will it sleep?" asked the angry bird from earlier.

"Fox," Tiny corrected. "His name is Fox."

The bird puffed up its feathers and huffed. "Where will *Fox* sleep?"

"Under the garden shed, beyond Frog's Hollow," said Tiny.

"As long as he doesn't come near *our* tree."

After the other animals left, Fox turned to Frog and Squirrel.

"I'm sorry for trying to eat you, Frog," he said, bowing his head.

"That's okay," said Frog. "I take it as a compliment."

"And I'm sorry I ate your fruit, Squirrel," said Fox.

Oh no, thought Tiny, wishing Fox hadn't been so truthful.

"WHAT?" said Squirrel. "It was *you*? I knew it! I knew it all along. And no one believed me, did they? They always—"

Squirrel's long rant was interrupted by the school bell. Tiny and the school garden animals dispersed for their daily activities, just as the children gathered in the playground, ready for their first break of the day.

And Fox – tired from his long journey to the school garden, and meeting lots of new friends – settled down for a long and peaceful sleep.

Aisha Bushby was born in the Middle East and now lives in the UK. When she's not reading or writing stories, she likes playing cosy video games, watching animated films, and working on her miniature house.

Kübra Teber lives in Ayvalık, Turkey. She likes reading, travelling, walking, finding antiques in flea markets and nature. She loves picnics most of all.

Find out how Tiny's adventures began in

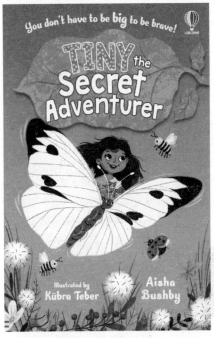

"Gorgeous... a very modern story with a wonderful inclusive message about caring for the world and those around you."
Holly Webb

And look out for her new adventure

With thanks to...

The Society of Authors for supporting
Aisha Bushby in the writing of this book with
their Authors' Foundation Grant.

Gareth Collinson
Sarah Cronin
Safae El-Ouahabi
Jessica Feichtlbauer
Anne Finnis
Beth Gardner
Helen Greathead
Alice Moloney
Will Steele
Kübra Teber
Claire Wilson

And everyone else who has
supported this book.